BUGS BUNNY™
Too Many Ca[rrots]

by Jean Lewis

illustrated by Peter Alvarado and Bob Totten

A Golden Book • New York
Western Publishing Company, Inc., Racine, Wisconsin 53404

Western Publishing Company, Inc., offers a wide variety of children's videos, tapes, and games.
For information, write to:
Western Publishing Company, Inc.
1220 Mound Avenue
Racine, WI 53404

Bugs Bunny smacked his lips. "Petunia," he said, "your plum preserves are just peachy!"

"Thank you, Bugs," said Petunia. "I hope the jam judges at the fair tomorrow agree with you."

Bugs was very busy. He was too lazy to enter the County Fair contests himself, but he loved giving orders to everyone else.

Bugs leaned out the kitchen window. "Porky, keep going!" he shouted. "You've got thirty-eight more seconds to do push-ups!"

"Poor Porky," sighed Petunia. "Do you *really* think he can swing that heavy hammer hard enough to ring the bell and win the prize?"

"Sure, if he wants to win badly enough," Bugs replied. Setting his stopwatch, he looked out the window again, then blew his whistle. "Take only a ten-second break before you start jogging!" he reminded Porky.

Just then Little Cicero ran in, demanding, "Petunia, I need another egg!"

"That's three eggs you've broken," scolded Petunia.

"I have to have eggs to practice with so I can win the race tomorrow," Cicero explained.

"What race?" asked Bugs.

"The egg-and-spoon race at the fair," said Cicero, reaching for the last egg in the carton.

"We'll hard-boil it first," suggested Bugs, putting the egg into a pan of water on the stove. "Then if it falls off your spoon, it'll just crack."

"But it's more fun when they break!" Cicero protested, watching his egg in the pan.

"Thank you, Bugs." Petunia laughed as Bugs bounded out the door, again blowing his whistle.

"It *can't* be ten seconds *yet!*" groaned Porky.

"It was ten seconds ten seconds ago," said Bugs. "On your feet—go! Be back in five and a half minutes. No stops! I'm timing you!"

As Porky jogged down the road, Bugs stretched out under a tree. He was just dozing off, when a familiar voice called over the fence, "What race are *you* trying to win?"

"What's up, doc?" called Bugs, looking over the fence at Elmer Fudd's garden. "Hey, your carrots are up! Would you like me to taste-test them?"

Reluctantly, Elmer handed him one. "I'm hoping to sell the whole crop at the fair tomorrow."

"Yummy," said Bugs, reaching for another carrot.

"Only one to a taste-tester," said Elmer. "And don't tell me you're practicing for a carrot-eating contest."

"Wish I'd thought of that." Bugs grinned. "I *never* get enough carrots."

"The pie-eating contest is the only eating event at the fair," said Elmer.

"And Uncle Hogitall always wins." Bugs was remembering other fairs.

"Why don't *you* challenge him?" Elmer asked. "With your appetite, you might beat him."

Bugs thought it over. "Well, I haven't any jams to enter or crops to sell—"

"And you're too lazy to get into shape," Elmer added.

"But my appetite is *always* in shape," bragged Bugs. "Thanks for the suggestion, doc. When Porky gets back, tell him to chin himself eighteen times on the crab apple tree. I'm off to sign up for the pie-eating contest!"

But when Bugs got to the fairground, he found that
the contest had been canceled.

"It's an outrage!" thundered Uncle Hogitall.

"You've won for eight years straight," snapped
Judge Turtle. "This year, nobody has challenged you,
so we're canceling the contest."

"Wait!" said Bugs. "I challenge Uncle Hogitall—
if I get to choose the kind of pie we eat."

"Don't you like blueberry pie?" asked the judge.

"I like carrot pie better," Bugs answered, smiling
hungrily.

"You want us to eat *carrot pies* for the contest?"
rumbled Uncle Hogitall.

"If it's okay with you, Judge Turtle, and the champ here," added Bugs, draping a friendly arm around Uncle Hogitall's shoulder.

After they agreed, Bugs signed up for the contest.

Next day, when the fair opened, an excited crowd gathered around a table stacked high with carrot pies. Would Bugs Bunny be able to outeat the all-time champion, Uncle Hogitall?

The champ arrived first. He sat down, tied a big napkin around his neck, and picked up a fork.

Then Bugs came, waved to the crowd, greeted Uncle Hogitall, tied on a napkin, and picked up a fork.

"Start eating!" shouted Judge Turtle.

"It's really unfair," murmured Bugs happily, chomping on his third pie. "I'm so *wild* about carrots!"

Then he noticed Uncle Hogitall smacking his lips over his *fourth* carrot pie.

"Better than blueberries!" commented the champ.

Meanwhile, Little Cicero easily won the egg-and-spoon race.

And Bugs and Uncle Hogitall kept eating.

Petunia proudly accepted a blue ribbon from the jam judges for her peachy plum preserves.

And Bugs and Uncle Hogitall ate on.

"*BONG!*" Porky swung the hammer, rang the bell, and won first prize for the highest score.

And Bugs and Uncle Hogitall each started on his *eighteenth* carrot pie.

"Must be something special about carrot pies," said Judge Turtle. "Fourteen blueberry pies are the most anybody's ever eaten before."

(And that was why Elmer Fudd sold *all* of his carrot crop. His customers wanted to bake carrot pies!)

In the middle of his nineteenth pie, Uncle Hogitall untied his napkin and laid down his fork with a sigh. "I know when I'm licked," he said.

Judge Turtle raised Bugs Bunny's arm. "The winner and new champion pie-eater!" he announced.

The crowd roared, and Bugs hiccupped. For once in his life, he didn't want to see another carrot.

But his grateful friends didn't realize this.

Porky and Petunia were the first to visit Bugs after he got home. "It was your training that helped me win," said Porky.

"After you called my plum preserves 'peachy,' I added just a dab of peach," said Petunia. "*That's* what won me the blue ribbon."

Together, they handed Bugs a big box.

"I baked you a carrot cake," beamed Petunia.

"My favorite," said Bugs feebly. "Thank you."

When Elmer Fudd came calling, Bugs said, "I hear you sold *all* your carrots. Glad to hear it."

"Thanks to you, everyone wants carrot pies," said Elmer. "But I saved some, just for you—three bushels of the best ones!"

"Lovely," gulped Bugs. "Thanks, doc."

Later, when Bugs saw Little Cicero coming, he tried to hide behind the nearest tree. But he wasn't fast enough. The winner of the egg-and-spoon race handed him a brown paper bag.

Bugs peeked in. "Carrot candy!" he croaked. Then he lay down under the nearest tree to think about something very strange: *Too many carrots are too many carrots,* he realized, even for the greatest carrot-eater of them all!